Illustrated by Ken McKie
Re-written by Ann McKie

© 2005 Alligator Books Limited
Gadd House, Arcadia Avenue
London N3 2JU

Printed in China

Contents

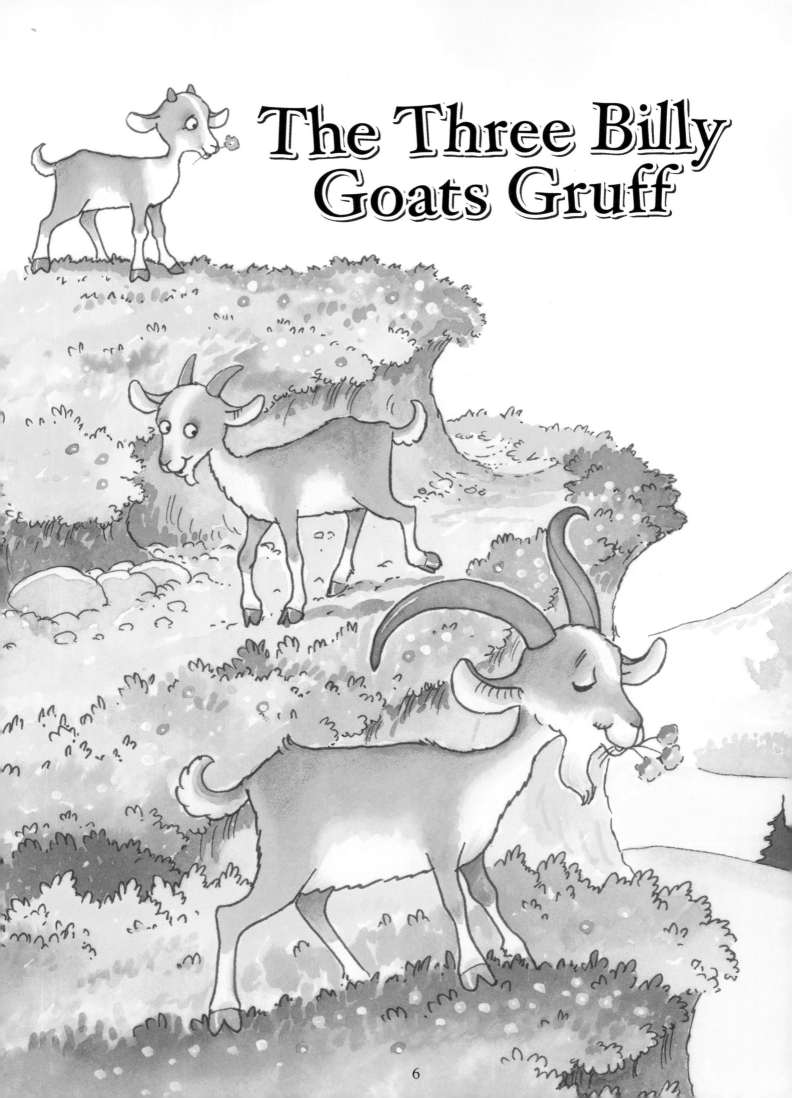

The Three Billy Goats Gruff

Once upon a time there were three billy goats. First there was the little billy goat Gruff, who was the smallest of the three.

Then there was the middle billy goat Gruff, who was bigger than the little billy goat Gruff, but not as big as the great big billy goat Gruff.

And he was, as you can see, the biggest of them all!

Now these billy goats lived in a tiny village at the foot of a high mountain.

Every year during spring and summer, the three billy goats Gruff left their tiny village and went to stay up on the hillside nearby.

All day long they nibbled the juicy green grass that grew there, and by night they slept underneath the stars.

Some days the three billy goats Gruff crossed the river to the other side of the valley, where the grass was even greener and juicier and full of sweet-smelling wild flowers.

Now the bridge over the river was very rickety-rackety. It swayed and creaked and went wibbly-wobbly.

"Perhaps someone will mend it one fine day," said the three billy goats Gruff every time they went trip-trapping across.

But when winter came along and snow covered the juicy green grass, the three billy goats Gruff said goodbye to the hillside, and went back to live in their tiny village at the foot of the high mountain.

So every year before the weather got too cold and the snow was too deep, the three billy goats Gruff trotted home down the mountain track.

The folks in the village were delighted to see them, especially the children. For it was their job to look after the three billy goats Gruff during the long months of winter.

Sometimes the children gave them oats to nibble from a basket, and barley from a big brass bucket.

The little billy goat Gruff, as you can see, would nibble anything that came his way!

But the three billy goats Gruff were happiest of all when the children brought them sweet-smelling hay. It reminded them of the juicy green grass that grew on the hillside in springtime.

And through the long dark winter nights, when the three billy goats Gruff were nice and warm and cosy in the barn, the children would listen to stories.

When the shutters were closed tight and the fire was burning brightly, that was the time the children wanted to hear about...TROLLS!

Now there are trolls with claws and rows of teeth!
There are trolls with horns and great big feet!
Some of them are scaly! Some of them are hairy!
But every single troll is...BIG, BAD AND SCARY!

The children listened to tales of trolls until it was past their bedtime.

"Goodnight and beware of the big bad trolls," they whispered sleepily as they went off to bed.

They hide under bridges,
In dark caves and holes.
Don't go up the mountain,
For fear of the TROLLS!

Now the three billy goats Gruff never heard the tales that were told about the trolls on dark winter nights.

Which was just as well perhaps!

On winter nights, as soon as darkness fell, all the animals in the warm cosy barn settled down to sleep.

The three billy goats Gruff closed their eyes and dreamed of spring, when the juicy green grass would grow on the hillside once more.

Then one very special morning, as the three billy goats Gruff came out of the barn...something felt different!

Birds were whistling, bees were humming and a sunbeam tickled the little billy goat Gruff's nose...SPRING HAD COME AT LAST!

"I can smell spring!" and the middle billy goat Gruff sighed as he sniffed the fresh air.

"It must be the new juicy green grass on the hillside you can smell!" said the great big billy goat Gruff.

So, without wasting a single moment, the three of them trotted out of the tiny village, and turned up the narrow path that led to the hillside.

When the three billy goats Gruff saw the new grass, it
made them feel hungry, and they began to nibble the fresh
shoots straight away.

They chomped and they munched, they chewed and they
crunched all morning long, until every single bit of the
juicy green grass had vanished.

"Where's it all gone?" gasped the little billy goat Gruff as
he stared at the ground.

"We've eaten it, I'm afraid!" said the middle billy goat
Gruff sadly.

"Look across the river!" cried the great big billy goat
Gruff. "There's a whole hillside covered with new juicy
green grass over there!"

The three billy goats Gruff could hardly wait to cross over the bridge and get to the new juicy green grass on the other side.

"I wonder if the bridge is still rickety-rackety?" asked the little billy goat Gruff as they rushed down to the river.

"I wonder if the bridge still sways and creaks and goes wibbly-wobbly?" asked the middle billy goat Gruff.

"I wonder if our hooves still go trip-trap every time we cross the bridge?" asked the great big billy goat Gruff.

"I'm the smallest! I'll go first!" called the little billy goat Gruff. "Then we'll find out!"

And off he went.

Now the three billy goats Gruff didn't know that during the long cold dark months of winter, a BIG BAD TROLL had come to live beneath the rickety-rackety bridge.

The instant he heard the little billy goat Gruff's small hooves trip-trapping across the wibbly-wobbly wooden planks, the big bad troll leapt out from under the rickety-rackety bridge.

He raged! He roared! He showed his claws!

He gnashed his pointed teeth!

"I'll eat anyone I catch trip-trapping across my bridge!" he growled fiercely.

The little billy goat Gruff stood quite still. He did not shake! He did not quake! He did not scream or shiver!

Instead he looked at the big bad troll and said, "My brother is much bigger than me. He'll make a better supper!"

So the big bad troll let the little billy goat Gruff go. And he went trip-trapping across the rickety-rackety bridge to the other side.

And there he stayed munching the juicy green grass as he waited for his brothers.

Next to cross the rickety-rackety bridge was the middle billy goat Gruff, who was bigger than the little billy goat Gruff, but not as big as the great big billy goat Gruff.

The very instant the big bad troll heard the middle billy goat's hooves trip-trapping across the wibbly-wobbly wooden planks, he leapt out from under the rickety-rackety bridge.

He raged! He roared! He showed his claws! He gnashed his pointed teeth!

"I'll eat anyone I catch trip-trapping across my bridge!" he growled fiercely.

The middle billy goat Gruff stood quite still. He didn't shake! He didn't quake! He didn't scream or shiver!

Instead he looked at the big bad troll and said, "My brother is much bigger than me. He'll make a better supper!"

So the big bad troll let the middle billy goat Gruff go. And he went trip-trapping across the rickety-rackety bridge to the other side.

And there he stayed munching the juicy green grass as he waited for his great big brother.

Now the big bad troll had made such a din, and hollered so loudly, that the great big billy goat Gruff realised what was happening.

And he knew just what to do!

The instant the big bad troll heard the great big billy goat Gruff's hooves on the wibbly-wobbly wooden planks, he leapt up onto the rickety-rackety bridge.

Then he opened his mouth wide and yelled, "You're big enough for my supper!"

"Oh no, I'm not!" snorted the great big billy goat Gruff.

Then he put down his huge sharp horns and he charged CRASH! BANG! WHAM!

The big bad troll whizzed high into the air, then flew over the mountains roaring and hollering. Where he landed, I can not tell, but he never came back again!

When the folks in the tiny village learned that the big bad troll had gone for ever, they wanted to thank the billy goats Gruff for being so brave and clever.

So they decided to celebrate.

It was the children's idea to have a grand picnic in honour of the three billy goats Gruff.

And everybody agreed.

So the next afternoon, (when the rickety-rackety bridge had been mended at last!) everyone trooped over the river to the hillside.

The three billy goats Gruff ate plenty of oats from a basket, and lots of barley from a brass bucket.

And the big bad troll, wherever he landed, must have told all the other trolls...never, never, under any circumstances whatsoever, go near the three billy goats Gruff!

The End

The Gingerbread Man

Once there lived an old man and woman and a little boy who all lived together in a country cottage. The old woman had been baking bread, cakes and sweet crunchy biscuits all morning. She had a bit of dough left over, so she decided to make a Gingerbread Man.

   The little boy was very keen to help. Straight away he
rolled up his sleeves, and very carefully, he gave the
Gingerbread Man currants for eyes, a bright red cherry
nose, a smiley orange slice mouth and three buttons made
of fat juicy raisins.
   The old woman popped the Gingerbread Man into the
oven to bake, then she went outside to talk to the old man
in the garden.
   All of a sudden, the oven door burst open and out leapt
the Gingerbread Man. To the little boy's amazement, he ran
across the kitchen floor and out of the open door.

The little boy could hardly believe his eyes as the Gingerbread Man raced down the garden path.

"Look at our Gingerbread Man!" yelled the little boy. "He's running away!"

"Be quick and catch him before he reaches the garden gate!" cried the old man.

"I'll grab him, then we'll eat him at once!" shouted the old woman.

So the old woman, the old man and the little boy all began to chase after the Gingerbread Man.

But the Gingerbread Man was far too quick for them. He'd escaped from the hot oven and now he was free as a bird.

As he ran through the gate and down the lane, the Gingerbread Man laughed and yelled at the top of his voice.

"Run! Run! As fast as you can! You can't catch me, I'm the Gingerbread Man!"

A snappy spotted dog that lived at the end of the lane, saw the runaway Gingerbread Man and joined in the chase.

When the Gingerbread Man saw the snappy spotted dog, he ran faster than ever.

"If I catch you first, I'll gobble you up, I promise!" barked the snappy spotted dog.

When the old man, the old woman and the little boy heard this, they ran faster too. They didn't want to lose their tasty golden Gingerbread Man with the red cherry nose, the currant eyes and juicy raisin buttons.

So they carried on down the lane chasing after the Gingerbread Man.

A hungry black crow flying overhead saw the Gingerbread Man, and swooped down hoping to take a big bite. But the Gingerbread Man was far too quick for him, and jumped out of his way.

"I've outrun an old man, an old woman, a little boy, a snappy spotted dog...and now you!" the Gingerbread Man yelled to the crow.

"Run! Run! As fast as you can! You can't catch me, I'm the Gingerbread Man!"

At the end of the lane was a field where three mowers were busy cutting corn, and raking it into neat piles to dry.

When they saw the Gingerbread Man running past, they stopped working at once and joined in the chase.

"Stop little Gingerbread Man!" cried one of the mowers. "You look tasty enough to eat for our lunch."

"I'll eat his head!" puffed the first mower.

"I'll eat his arms!" panted the second.

"And I'll eat both his legs!" gasped the third.

But the Gingerbread Man didn't stop. He skipped and danced as he crossed the corn field, and he called back to the three mowers...

"Run! Run! As fast as you can! You can't catch me, I'm the Gingerbread Man!"

The midday sun was so hot, and the mowers felt so tired, they sat down in the shade to eat their lunch. They ate bread and cheese, but no tasty Gingerbread Man, of course!

How the old man, the old woman, the little boy and the snappy spotted dog longed to stop and rest in the shade, but they were all determined to carry on and catch the Gingerbread Man.

They ran up hill and down dale. They ran over bridges, through woods and across fields. Everyone had come so far, they were all exhausted and quite out of breath.

But the Gingerbread Man wasn't tired at all, and he sang at the top of his voice as he raced along.

"Run! Run! As fast as you can! You can't catch me, I'm the Gingerbread Man!"

And he was absolutely right. The Gingerbread Man had run so fast, he had left everyone far behind.

On and on ran the Gingerbread man. After a little while he came to a farm. Standing by the gate were two fat little piglets looking very forlorn.

"The farmer is late with our dinner," moaned one little piglet.

"And we are both very hungry," groaned the other one.

Then they began to squeal at the top of their voices. "We want our dinner! We want our dinner!"

Suddenly both little piglets stopped and looked at the Gingerbread Man. "Dinner!" they squealed, and began to chase after him.

But the Gingerbread Man didn't care one little bit.

"An old man, an old woman, a little boy, a snappy spotted dog and three mowers can't catch me," boasted the Gingerbread Man, "and you two fat little piglets never will!" Then off he ran.

The two little piglets trotted back to the farm to find some dinner.

"He'll get gobbled up one fine day!" said one of the piglets.

"Hope so!" said the other.

As the Gingerbread Man hurried on, he crossed a meadow where a pony was grazing. When the pony noticed the Gingerbread Man, he trotted across.

"Where are you going in such a hurry?" asked the pony.

"An old man, an old woman, a little boy and a snappy spotted dog are all trying to catch me," laughed the Gingerbread Man. "But I'm far too fast for them!"

Now the pony liked to eat grass and carrots and hay, but he loved to eat sweet crunchy biscuits even more.

"If they can't catch you, I will, and I'll gobble you up in a couple of bites!" said the pony and he began to chase the Gingerbread Man round and round the meadow.

But try as he might, the pony couldn't keep up with the speedy Gingerbread Man.

"Run! Run! As fast as you can! You can't catch me, I'm the Gingerbread Man!" Then he ran out of the meadow and scrambled up onto a river bank.

The Gingerbread Man gazed down in dismay, the river was wide and the water looked deep.

"Oh dear me!" the Gingerbread Man sighed. "Very soon, the old man, the old woman, the little boy, the snappy spotted dog and the pony will catch up with me...and I can't swim."

Now the Gingerbread Man hadn't noticed a sly red fox hiding in the reeds by the river.

"My dear Gingerbread Man," called the fox, trying very hard not to lick his lips. "Are you in some kind of trouble?"

"I'm in a bit of a hurry," replied the Gingerbread Man. "I need to cross the river as quick as possible, and I'm afraid I can't swim!"

"No problem," smiled the crafty fox. "I happen to be a very strong swimmer. Jump onto my back and I will carry you across with pleasure."

When they reached the middle of the river, the fox asked the Gingerbread Man to climb onto his head, just in case he got wet.

"My dear Gingerbread Man," called the fox as he swam along. "The water is getting much deeper now. I'm afraid you might drown."

"What shall I do?" the poor Gingerbread Man wailed.

"Could you possibly climb onto my nose?" asked the sly old fox.

As soon as he did, the fox tossed him up into the air, opened his mouth wide, and gobbled up the Gingerbread Man in one bite.

And that was the end of him.

Nobody could catch the Gingerbread Man, not the old man, or the old woman, or the little boy, or the snappy spotted dog, or the three mowers, or the hungry little piglets or the pony.

But the clever old fox did, didn't he?

The End

Little Red Riding Hood

There was once a little girl who lived with her parents in a cottage on the edge of a large forest.

Her father was a woodcutter, and each morning he would go deep into the forest where he worked hard all day long chopping down trees.

For her birthday one year, the little girl's grandmother made her a red cloak with a hood to match. The little girl wore her beautiful cloak every time she went outside – and that is why she became known as Little Red Riding Hood.

One day when Little Red Riding Hood was playing in the garden, she heard her mother calling from the cottage.

"Your grandmother is not very well, and she has decided to stay in bed today. Perhaps you could take her something to cheer her up."

So together they packed a basket. They put in a freshly baked loaf of bread, some butter and a jar of strawberry jam.

Then Little Red Riding Hood laid a clean cloth on top of the basket, and she was ready to go to her grandmother's house.

Now Little Red Riding Hood's grandmother lived on the other side of the forest. So before she set off, her mother made the little girl promise never to stray from the path, and never to talk to strangers.

Little Red Riding Hood listened carefully, then off she went dressed in her special red cloak.

"Go straight to Grandmother's house, and remember to keep to the path!" her mother called as she watched her disappear into the forest.

Red Riding Hood was half way to her grandmother's house when a big grey wolf stepped out from behind a tree.

"Good morning, my dear. What a simply lovely red cloak you have on!" said the wolf, doing his best to look friendly.

When Little Red Riding Hood heard this, she forgot what her mother had told her, and she began to talk to the wolf.

"My grandmother made it for my birthday," said the little girl politely. "She is ill in bed now, and I am going to cheer her up!"

"How very kind, my dear," smiled the wolf trying not to show his sharp teeth.

"And what have you got in your basket for Grandmother?" the wolf asked Little Red Riding Hood.

"Freshly baked bread, golden butter and her favourite strawberry jam," she replied.

"How simply delicious," said the wolf licking his lips.

Can you believe that at that very moment, the wicked wolf was planning to gobble up Little Red Riding Hood, and her grandmother too, if he had half a chance!

"Where does your grandmother live?" asked the wicked wolf.

"Right at the end of this path on the far side of the forest," said Little Red Riding Hood as she walked along.

"Why not take some of these beautiful flowers to your grandmother?" suggested the wolf - for he was trying to delay Little Red Riding Hood as long as he could.

When the little girl saw the flowers growing by the path, she stopped at once and began to pick them.

Red Riding Hood was so busy, she never noticed the wolf bound off down the path towards her grandmother's house.

Perhaps the wolf knew a short cut through the trees, for in less time than it takes to tell, he was knocking on Grandmother's door.

"Who is it?" called the old lady from her bed.

"It's Little Red Riding Hood," whispered the wolf as softly as he could.

"Just lift up the latch and walk right in!" said the grandmother.

The big grey wolf rushed through the door, bounded into the bedroom and leapt onto Grandmother's bed.

When the poor old lady heard the wolf snarl, and saw his sharp pointed teeth, she threw back the bedclothes, jumped out of bed, ran outside and hid behind the woodshed.

Meanwhile, the wolf put on one of Grandmother's spare nightdresses and one of her frilly nightcaps. He even found a spare pair of glasses on a table by the bed.

"I feel these glasses suit me very well. I really do look like a grandmother!" and the wolf smiled as he admired himself in the mirror.

"When Little Red Riding Hood arrives, I shall gobble her up, and I'll eat her grandmother later!" and the wolf sniggered and snapped his teeth loudly.

Then he jumped into Grandmother's bed, and pulled the bedclothes up to his chin.

Before very long, Little Red Riding Hood came skipping up the path and knocked gently on her grandmother's door.

"Who is there?" croaked the wolf trying his best to sound like the old lady.

"It's Little Red Riding Hood come to cheer you up," the little girl replied.

"How strange grandmother sounds, perhaps she has a sore throat," Little Red Riding Hood thought to herself.

"How are you feeling today?" the little girl asked as she tiptoed across her grandmother's room. But when the little girl put down her basket and flowers, she jumped back in surprise.

"Just lift the latch and walk right in!" said the wolf.

"Why Grandmother, what big ears you have!" she cried.

"All the better to hear you with!" said the wolf in a deep voice. "Come closer my dear!"

So Little Red Riding Hood stepped a little closer to her grandmother's bed.

"Why Grandmother, what big eyes you have!" said the little girl staring at the wolf in her grandmother's silver glasses.

"All the better to see you with!" grinned the wolf. "Come closer my dear!"

So Little Red Riding Hood took one more step forward, and looked very carefully at the wolf in her grandmother's nightdress and frilly nightcap.

"Why Grandmother, what big teeth you have!" gasped Little Red Riding Hood.

"All the better to EAT you with!" snarled the wolf as he leapt out of bed.

"You're not my grandmother!" yelled Little Red Riding Hood.

"Indeed I'm not," growled the wolf. "I'm the big bad wolf, and I'm going to gobble you up!"

When she heard that, Little Red Riding Hood ran out of the room screaming at the top of her voice, with the wolf close behind her.

As she rushed out of the front door, she fell right into the arms of her father, the woodcutter.

He had been chopping down trees nearby, along with some of the other woodsmen. When he heard Little Red Riding Hood's screams, and saw Grandmother peeping from behind the woodshed, he guessed that something was wrong.

"The wolf is going to gobble me up," shrieked the little girl. "Look! He's right behind me!"

When the woodcutter saw the wolf running out of Grandmother's front door, he grabbed his sharp axe, ready to chop off the wolf's head.

When the wolf saw the woodcutter, he trembled with fright, and ran for his life.

"That wicked wolf must have gobbled up poor Grandmother," sobbed Little Red Riding Hood.

"No he hasn't!" smiled the little girl's father. "There she is. She's been hiding behind the woodshed all the time."

How happy everyone felt. Grandmother was safe, and feeling much better in spite of her fright. Little Red Riding Hood was safe too, thanks to her brave father.

The wicked wolf was gone forever, and would never return while the woodcutters were in the forest.

It was getting late so the woodcutters headed for home. No doubt they would tell their children that night, how they had chased a big bad wolf, who was dressed in a nightdress and frilly nightcap!

The End

The Ugly Duckling

It was a warm day in summer, and a mother duck was sitting all by herself on her nest at the far end of a pond. She felt rather lonely, for it seemed to her that she'd been there for ever.

At long last one of the eggs cracked open, and out popped a tiny duckling, then another and another. Before very long, there were six fluffy yellow ducklings doing their best to jump out of the nest.

Then she noticed that the biggest of her eggs hadn't hatched. So she settled down to keep the egg warm underneath her soft feathers.

While the mother duck waited, she watched her ducklings scurrying to and fro as they explored their new world.

"I do believe that the world is a great deal bigger than our pond," she quacked nodding her head wisely. "It stretches right up to the farmyard...and that's as far as it goes I think!"

It didn't take long before the big egg began to crack open, and a large grey bird with a huge head and a long neck came tumbling out of its shell.

"Oh my! Oh my!" quacked the mother duck.

"You don't look a bit like your brothers and sisters. I'm not even sure that you are a duckling at all!"

As soon as the other six ducklings heard all the noise, they scurried out of the reeds and gathered round the new arrival.

"Oh my!" said the mother duck with a sigh. "He does look rather funny, a bit strange, you might say."

"He's not like us!" cheeped the smallest of the six ducklings. Then the others joined in. "He's not even yellow!" "His head is too big!" "His feet are enormous!"

"His neck is long and skinny!" "AND HE'S UGLY!"

"Now, that is not so," said the mother duck. "He's not ugly, he's just different!"

But sad to say, from that day on, the poor duckling became known as the Ugly Duckling.

Mother duck was eager to show off her newly hatched family, so she led them down to the pond for their first swim.

When they reached the water's edge, the ducklings plopped in one by one, and soon they were swimming round in the water.

"Don't you dare come near us!" the six yellow ducklings shouted to the Ugly Duckling as they bobbed up and down near their mother.

"Why, he's the best swimmer of you all!" quacked the mother duck. "He may look different, but one day, he'll outshine every one of you!"

After a while, the mother duck led her ducklings across the pond and into the farmyard.

The geese and the rest of the birds gathered round and stared when they saw the Ugly Duckling.

"What is that?" hissed the farmyard gander rudely.

"He's the biggest of my new ducklings," the mother duck replied.

"He's the ugliest!" crowed the cockerel at the top of his voice.

The Ugly Duckling's six brothers and sisters cheeped with laughter, and the rest of the farmyard birds joined in.

Everyone was so unkind, it made the poor Ugly Duckling feel very unhappy.

As the weeks went by, the ducklings and their mother spent more and more time in the farmyard. The Ugly Duckling was pecked and hassled all day long.

"They tease me because I'm so ugly," thought the Ugly Duckling as he tried to get away from the other birds.

One morning a girl from the farmhouse came into the yard to feed the poultry.

"Get out of my way, you ugly creature!" and she threw grain from her bucket at the Ugly Duckling.

The duckling was so shocked, he tumbled through the hedge, and landed upside-down in a field full of sharp corn stalks.

The sparrows and finches that were perching on the branches fluttered up into the sky with fright.

"Everyone I meet is frightened of me because of the way I look," sighed the Ugly Duckling. "It must be because I am so ugly. I shall go far away from here and never come back again!"

So early next morning, he ran away from the cruel birds in the farmyard.

The Ugly Duckling travelled all day long. At last he came to a great open marsh where the wild ducks lived.

"You're not the prettiest of ducks!" quacked one of the drakes. "But you're welcome to stay here as long as you like," and away he flew.

Week after week the Ugly Duckling hid in the rushes all alone. Nobody bothered him, until one day, a hunting dog came sniffing round.

The wild ducks flew off at once. There were men on the marsh carrying guns, and the wild ducks knew not to stay.

When the hunting dog discovered the Ugly Duckling, he growled and bared his teeth, then he turned and ran off into the reeds.

"Even the dog thinks I'm ugly," said the duckling. "That is the reason he didn't bite me!"

It was autumn now, and the weather was getting colder day by day. It was time for the Ugly Duckling to leave the marsh and find somewhere away from the wind and the rain.

After a long search, he came upon a tumbledown cottage. It looked quite empty, so the duckling squeezed through a hole in the door where the wood had rotted away.

Once inside the cottage, he hid in a corner and fell
fast asleep.

When the Ugly Duckling woke up the next morning, he
was in for quite a surprise. An old woman lived there with
her cat and her hen and she found the duckling as soon as it
was light.

The old woman was delighted the duckling had come and
she begged him to stay. She thought he would lay plenty of
duck eggs for tea.

But her companions, the cat and the hen, had other ideas.
"I can catch mice! Can you?" snarled the cat.
The Ugly Duckling shook his head.
"I can lay eggs! Can you?" clucked the hen.
The Ugly Duckling shook his head again, for he had no idea how to lay an egg.
"The old woman will fatten you up and eat you for dinner, you ugly bird!" sneered the cat and the hen.

Their bullying went on and on and on. So after a while, although winter had arrived, the Ugly Duckling knew he had to move on.

So early one morning, before anyone in the cottage
was awake, he squeezed out of the door where the
wood had rotted away.

As the duckling walked through the day, snowflakes
began to fall. Then, at long last, he came to a quiet
lake. And there he stayed all alone. By day he swam
in the icy water, and when darkness fell he went to
sleep in the hollow of an old tree.

One evening as the sun was setting, and a mist was drifting across the lake, the Ugly Duckling looked up and saw a flock of beautiful birds passing overhead.

"How I wish I was one of those birds, then I could fly away with them and be happy for ever."

That night he stayed on the water dreaming of those wonderful birds. But by morning the lake had turned to ice. The poor duckling was frozen fast and couldn't move.

A farmer, who happened
to be passing by, freed the
poor bird and carried him
home in his thick jacket.

The farmhouse kitchen
was cosy and warm, and
the Ugly Duckling soon
thawed out. The farmer's
children were very young
and wanted to play with him.
It seemed like fun to them.

But the Ugly Duckling didn't know they were
just being friendly, he was frightened and tried to
get away.

He stumbled around the kitchen in panic, he knocked over the milk, fell into the flour and then ran across the butter.

The farmer's wife clapped her hands, the children screamed and the farmer chased him out of the door!

So the Ugly Duckling fled to the lake, and went back and hid in the hollow tree. He stayed there until the snow was gone and the ice had melted away.

Spring came at last! The weather was warm and sunny, and great flocks of birds returned to the lake. Winter was gone, and for the first time in his life the Ugly Duckling felt happy to be alive.

Boldly he swam into the middle of the lake, then he spread out his strong wings and soared high into the air...he could fly!

As he landed gracefully at the edge of the lake, he saw his reflection in the clear water. Looking back at him was a beautiful white bird.

He could hardly believe his eyes, for during the long months of winter, the Ugly Duckling had grown into a magnificent swan.

Very soon, the other swans on the lake came gliding across the water to make him welcome.

"Are you on your own?" asked one of the swans in the kindest way.

"Please come and live with us," said another.

No words can ever describe how happy this made the beautiful new swan feel.

The new swan's dreams had come true at last, and no one would ever call him ugly again.

The End